To all you bright sparks at Moulsham Junior School! K.G.

To Violet M. McQ

First edition for the United States, its territories and dependencies, the Philippine Republic, and Canada published in 2006 by Barron's Educational Series, Inc.

Originally published in 2006 by Hodder Children's Books, a division of Hodder Headline Limited, London
Text copyright © Kes Gray 2006.
Illustrations copyright © Mary McQuillan 2006.

The right of Kes Gray to be identified as the author and Mary McQuillan as the illustrator of this Work has been asserted by them in accordance with the Copyright, Designs and Patent Act 1988.

All inquiries should be addressed to:
Barron's Educational Series, Inc.
250 Wireless Boulevard
Hauppauge, New York 11788
www.barronseduc.com

ISBN-13: 978-0-7641-6008-0
ISBN-10: 0-7641-6008-7

Library of Congress Control No.: 2006920216

Printed in China
9 8 7 6 5 4 3 2 1

Twoo Twit

Written by
KES GRAY

Illustrated by
MARY McQUILLAN

BARRON'S

Twoo Twit certainly looked like an owl.
He had the eyes of an owl, the beak of
an owl, and the feathers of an owl.
But he had the brains of a fly!

"I thought owls were supposed
to be clever," said the fox cubs.
"They are," said their mom.
"So why does Twoo Twit keep crashing
into his tree?"
"He keeps forgetting the hole is around
the other side," said their mom.

"I thought owls were supposed to be wise,"
said the badger pups.
"They are," said their dad.

"Then why has Twoo Twit just perched
his bottom on that prickly bush?"
"He hasn't learned about thorns,"
said their dad.

"Aren't owls supposed
to be good at math?"
asked the bunnies.
"Most certainly," said
the mother rabbit.

"Then how come Twoo Twit gave the hawk two hundred and fifty blackberries for two beak sharpeners when they were only six blackberries each?"
"Because he's a noodle," said the mother hare.

SHOP

"He's a dandelion brain,"
said the weasel kittens.

"He's a mushroom head,"
said the partridge chicks.

It was true. Twoo Twit was without doubt the silliest
collection of feathers ever to take to the sky.

Every night Twoo Twit's mom would
put some blueberry sandwiches
in a bag and wave Twoo Twit
off to night school.

But Twoo Twit never ever went to school.

Sometimes he would fly to the farm
on the hill to play in the bales of hay.

Other times he would fly to the brook
and spend an entire night sending
twigs down the stream.

There were lots of places
Twoo Twit liked going.
Not one of them was school.

Tonight he had decided to go to the church tower to gaze at the twinkly lights of the town. He was hanging upside down from the bell, happily munching his sandwiches, when suddenly . . .

He was shaken to the roots of his feathers.

CLANG CLO TWOOOOOOO!!

"What's happening?" he squawked.

DING

NG

DONG

Twit!!!

"Make it stop!" he screeched.

But it didn't stop. It wouldn't stop.
The clangs kept clinging and
clonging, and the dings kept
dinging and donging.

Finally, thankfully, after two long, long, ding dong hours, the church bell stopped ringing and Twoo Twit stopped wobbling.

BELL
RINGING
CONTEST
TONIGHT

With a squeak and a squawk,
Twoo Twit raced back to the forest.

"But couldn't you read the sign?"
said the animals. "There was
a big sign in the churchyard."

"Of course I could read the sign," said Twoo Twit. "I have better eyesight than all of you."

"Well if you could read the sign, tell us what it said then," said the magpie chicks.

"Er... it said, THIS IS THE CHURCH," guessed Twoo Twit.

"No it didn't," said the fox cubs.

"THE PASTOR LIVES HERE?"
guessed Twoo Twit.

"No," said
the partridge chicks.

"Er ... it said, DECENT ORGAN
PLAYER NEEDED," guessed Twoo Twit.

All the forest children shook their heads.

"It said, **BELL RINGING CONTEST TONIGHT,'** chuckled the fawns.

"Eight till ten," giggled the badger pups.

"Sandwiches provided," laughed the weasel kittens.

"You can't read at all, can you?" hooted the animals.

With the sound of forest laughter ringing in his ears, Twoo Twit flew home to his mom and dad and hung his head in shame. He'd never felt like such a cuckoo brain before.

The following night a most unusual sound was heard in the forest. It was as loud as a church bell and as clear as a choir solo, but it came from the school.

"HERE MISS!" shouted Twoo Twit.